IR

THE LIVER
A GRAPHIC NOVEL TOUR

written by
Joeming Dunn
illustrated by
Rod Espinosa

magic wagon

visit us at
www.abdopublishing.com

Published by Magic Wagon, a division of the ABDO Group, 8000 West 78th Street, Edina, Minnesota 55439. Copyright © 2010 by Abdo Consulting Group, Inc. International copyrights reserved in all countries. All rights reserved. No part of this book may be reproduced in any form without written permission from the publisher.

Graphic Planet™ is a trademark and logo of Magic Wagon.

Printed in the United States.

 Manufactured with paper containing at least 10% post-consumer waste

Text by Joeming Dunn
Illustrated by Rod Espinosa
Colored and lettered by Rod Espinosa
Edited by Stephanie Hedlund
Interior layout and design by Antarctic Press
Cover art by Rod Espinosa
Cover design by Neil Klinepier

Library of Congress Cataloging-in-Publication Data

Dunn, Joeming W.
  The liver : a graphic novel tour / by Joeming Dunn ; illustrated by Rod Espinosa.
      p. cm. -- (Graphic adventures. The human body)
  Includes index.
  ISBN 978-1-60270-687-3
  1. Liver--Juvenile literature. 2. Graphic novels--Juvenile literature. I. Espinosa, Rod, ill. II. Title.
  QP185.D86 2010
  612.3'5--dc22
                              2009017853

TABLE of CONTENTS

Meet the Explorers.................................4

Liver and Onions! 5

The Liver: A Diagram...........................28

Fun Facts...29

Glossary 30

Web Sites...30

About the Author..................................31

About the Illustrator............................31

Index..32

Meet the Explorers

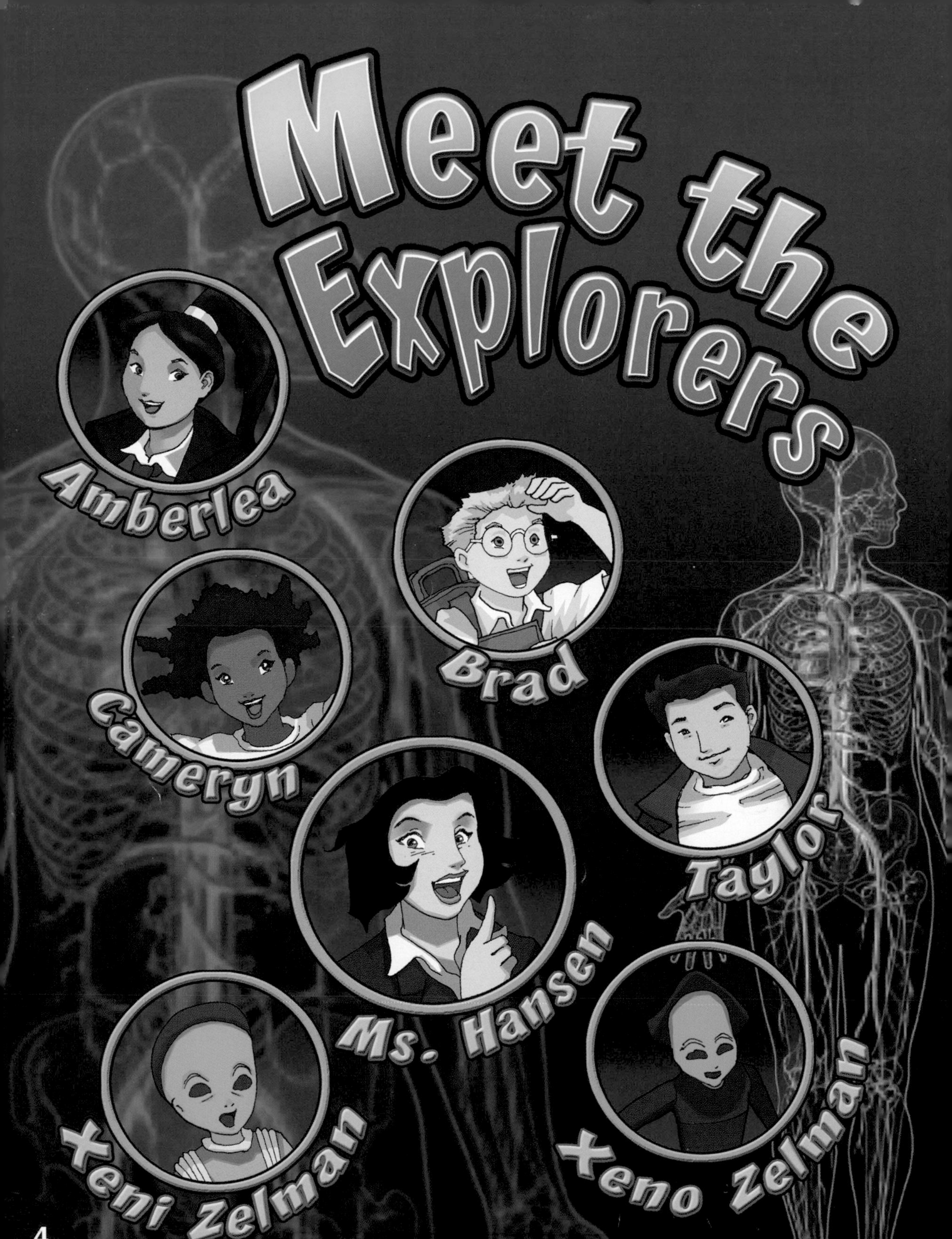
Amberlea
Brad
Cameryn
Taylor
Ms. Hansen
Xeni Zelman
Xeno Zelman

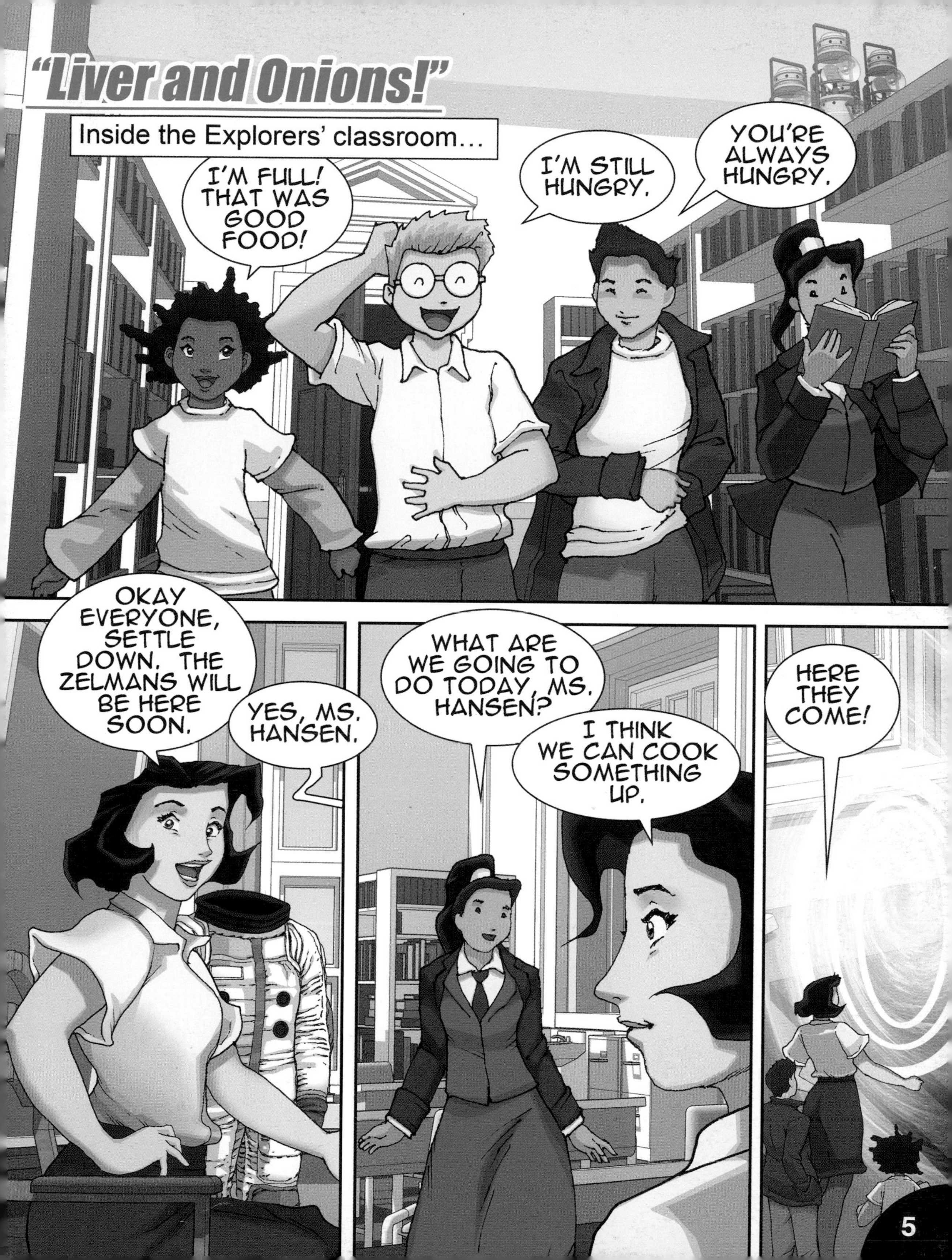

"Liver and Onions!"
Inside the Explorers' classroom…
I'M FULL! THAT WAS GOOD FOOD!
I'M STILL HUNGRY.
YOU'RE ALWAYS HUNGRY.
OKAY EVERYONE, SETTLE DOWN. THE ZELMANS WILL BE HERE SOON.
YES, MS. HANSEN.
WHAT ARE WE GOING TO DO TODAY, MS. HANSEN?
I THINK WE CAN COOK SOMETHING UP.
HERE THEY COME!

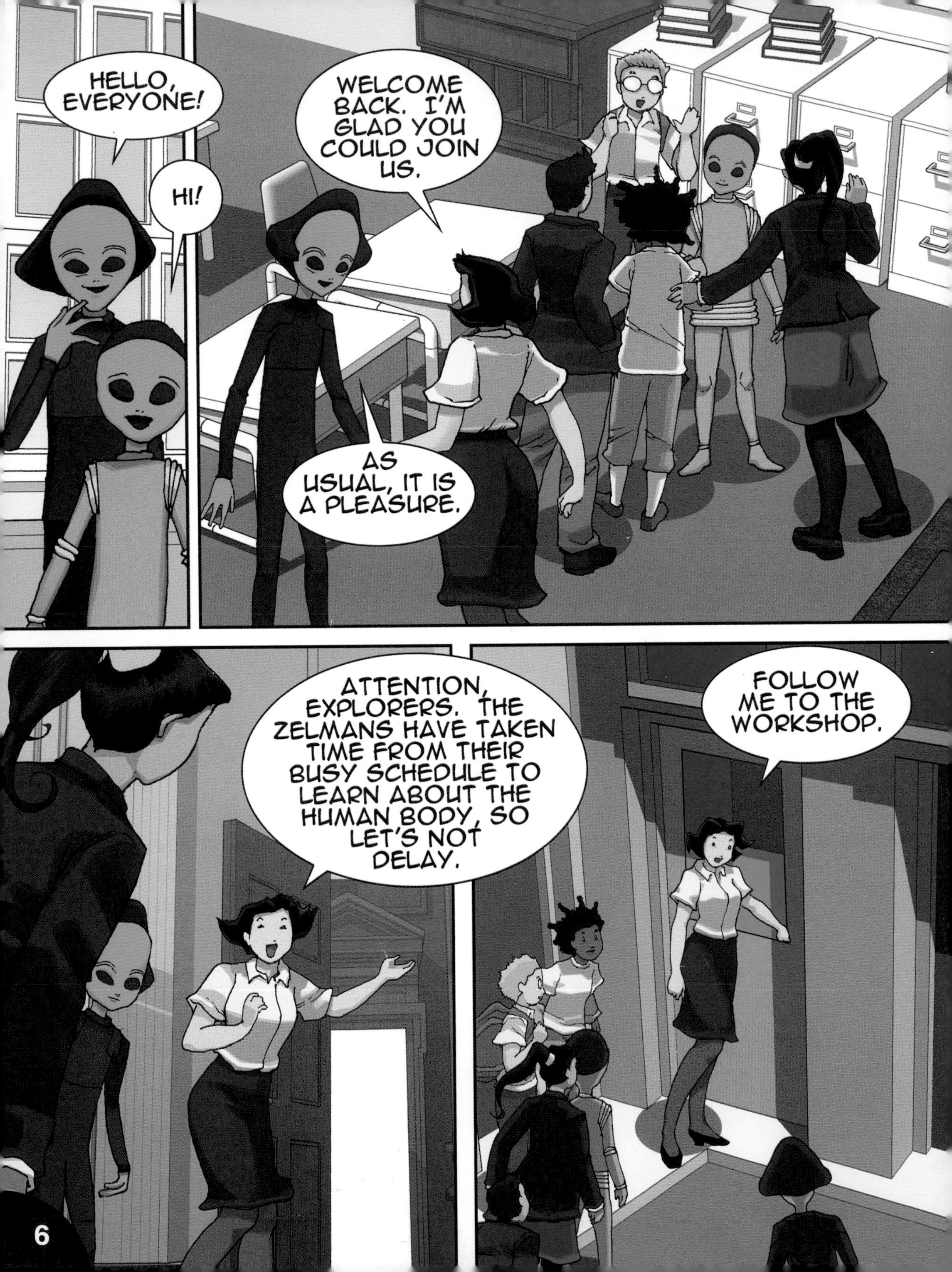
HELLO, EVERYONE!
HI!
WELCOME BACK. I'M GLAD YOU COULD JOIN US.
AS USUAL, IT IS A PLEASURE.
ATTENTION, EXPLORERS. THE ZELMANS HAVE TAKEN TIME FROM THEIR BUSY SCHEDULE TO LEARN ABOUT THE HUMAN BODY, SO LET'S NOT DELAY.
FOLLOW ME TO THE WORKSHOP.

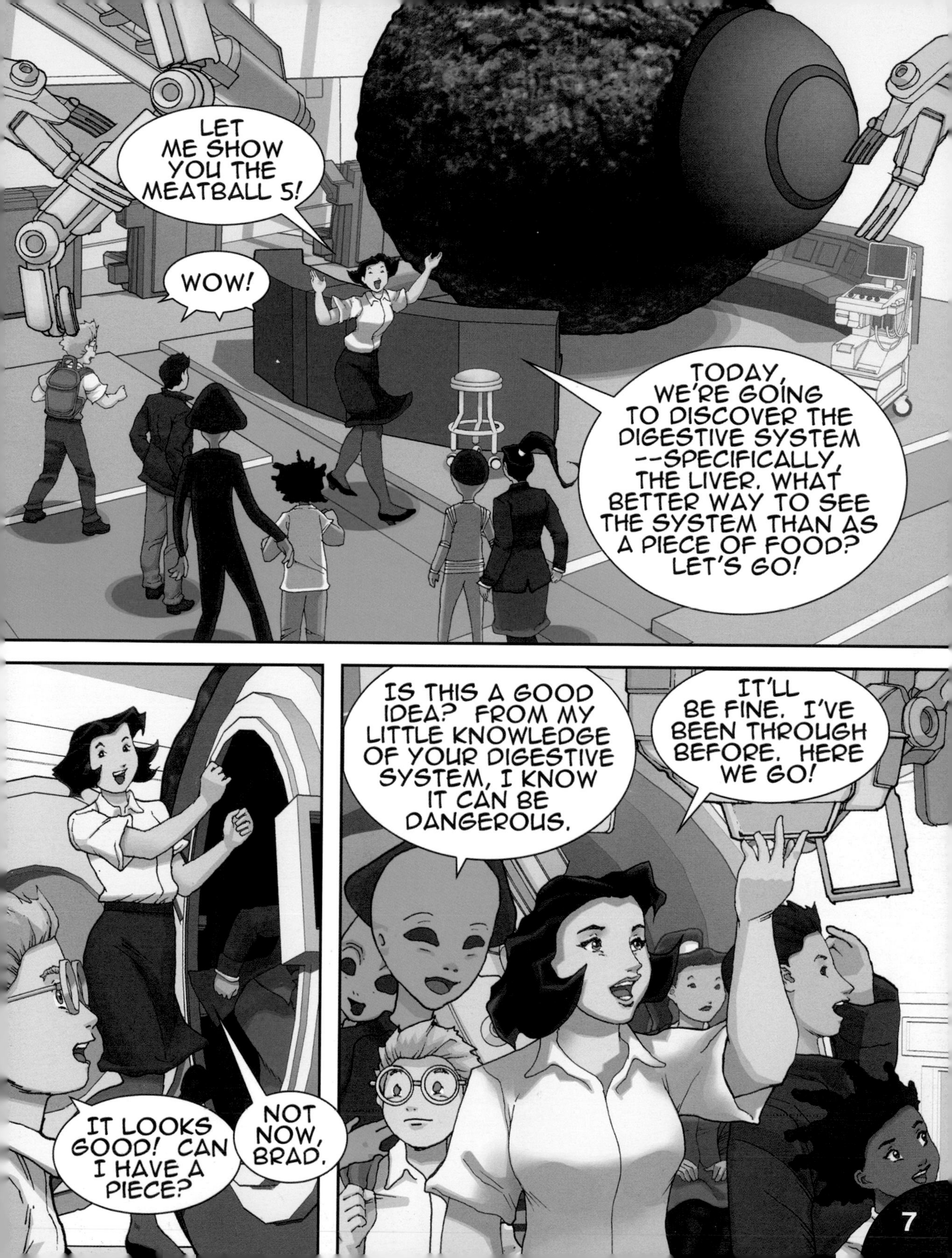
LET ME SHOW YOU THE MEATBALL 5!
WOW!
TODAY, WE'RE GOING TO DISCOVER THE DIGESTIVE SYSTEM --SPECIFICALLY, THE LIVER. WHAT BETTER WAY TO SEE THE SYSTEM THAN AS A PIECE OF FOOD? LET'S GO!
IT LOOKS GOOD! CAN I HAVE A PIECE?
NOT NOW, BRAD.
IS THIS A GOOD IDEA? FROM MY LITTLE KNOWLEDGE OF YOUR DIGESTIVE SYSTEM, I KNOW IT CAN BE DANGEROUS.
IT'LL BE FINE. I'VE BEEN THROUGH BEFORE. HERE WE GO!

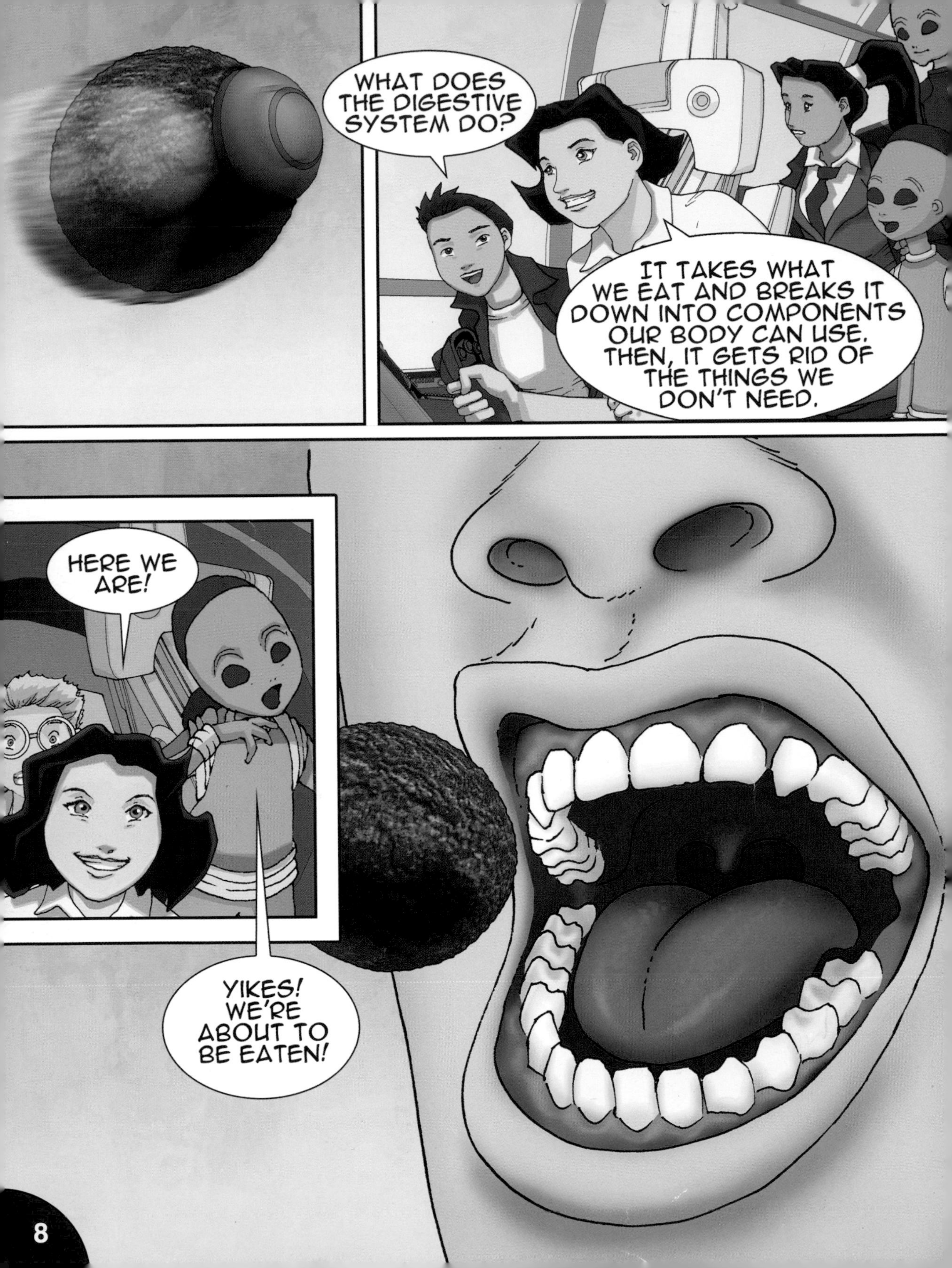
WHAT DOES THE DIGESTIVE SYSTEM DO?
IT TAKES WHAT WE EAT AND BREAKS IT DOWN INTO COMPONENTS OUR BODY CAN USE. THEN, IT GETS RID OF THE THINGS WE DON'T NEED.
HERE WE ARE!
YIKES! WE'RE ABOUT TO BE EATEN!

EVERYONE OUT!

EWW! THE GROUND IS SO SOFT!

THAT'S BECAUSE WE'RE ON THE TONGUE.

THIS IS THE TONGUE, WHICH IS A BUNCH OF MUSCLES. THEY HELP MOVE YOUR FOOD AROUND THE MOUTH WHILE CHEWING.

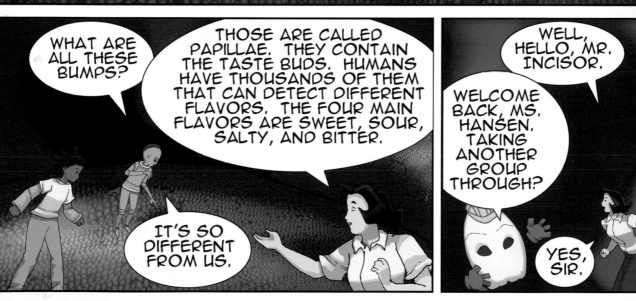

WHAT ARE ALL THESE BUMPS?

THOSE ARE CALLED PAPILLAE. THEY CONTAIN THE TASTE BUDS. HUMANS HAVE THOUSANDS OF THEM THAT CAN DETECT DIFFERENT FLAVORS. THE FOUR MAIN FLAVORS ARE SWEET, SOUR, SALTY, AND BITTER.

IT'S SO DIFFERENT FROM US.

WELL, HELLO, MR. INCISOR.

WELCOME BACK, MS. HANSEN. TAKING ANOTHER GROUP THROUGH?

YES, SIR.

EXPLORERS, THIS IS MR. INCISOR. HE IS IN CHARGE OF THE TEETH, WHICH ARE USED FOR THE BEGINNING OF DIGESTION. THEY BREAK DOWN THE BITES OF FOOD WE EAT INTO SMALLER PARTS.

UHH... MS. HANSEN--

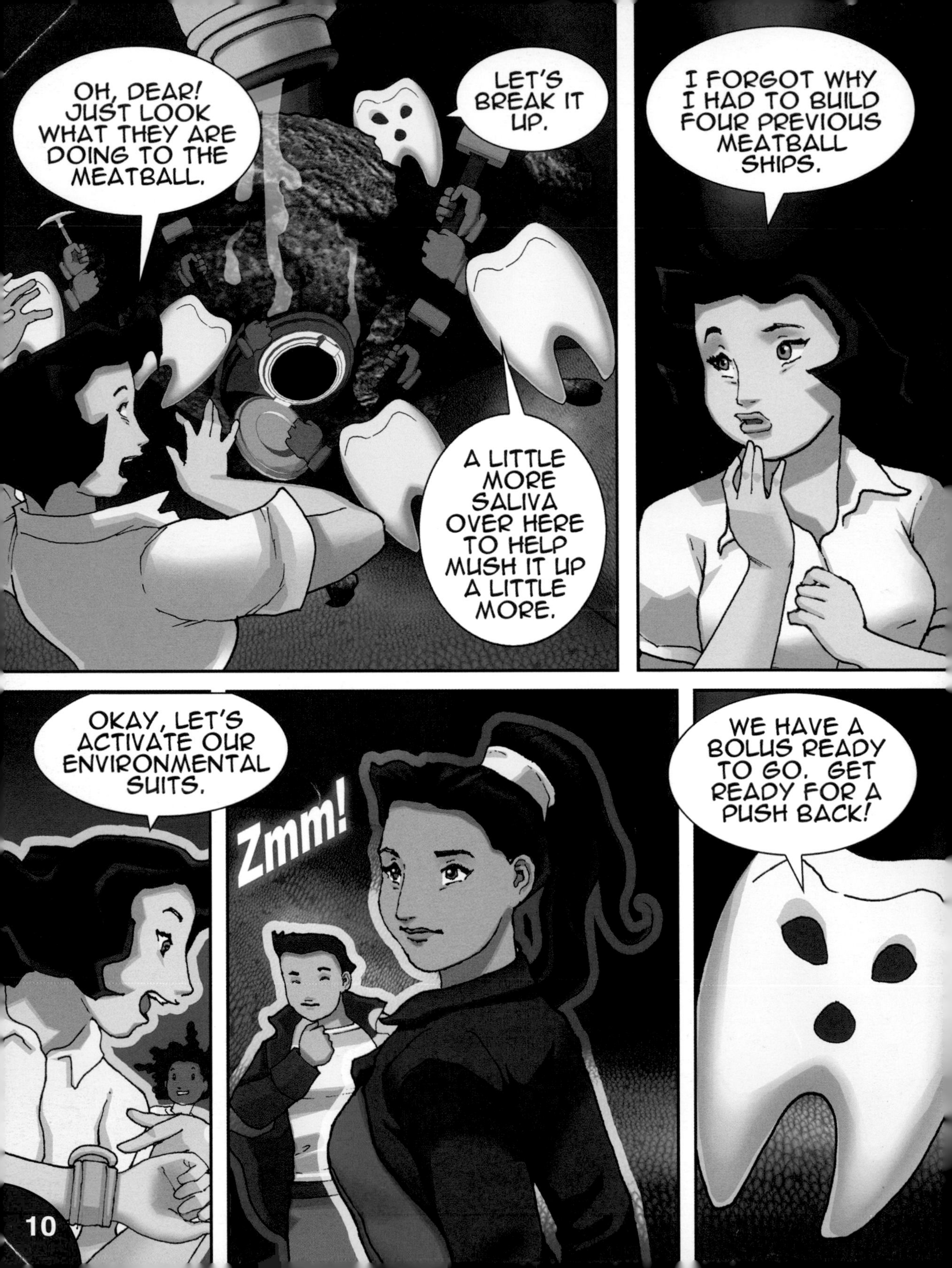
OH, DEAR! JUST LOOK WHAT THEY ARE DOING TO THE MEATBALL.
LET'S BREAK IT UP.
A LITTLE MORE SALIVA OVER HERE TO HELP MUSH IT UP A LITTLE MORE.
I FORGOT WHY I HAD TO BUILD FOUR PREVIOUS MEATBALL SHIPS.
OKAY, LET'S ACTIVATE OUR ENVIRONMENTAL SUITS.
Zmm!
WE HAVE A BOLUS READY TO GO. GET READY FOR A PUSH BACK!

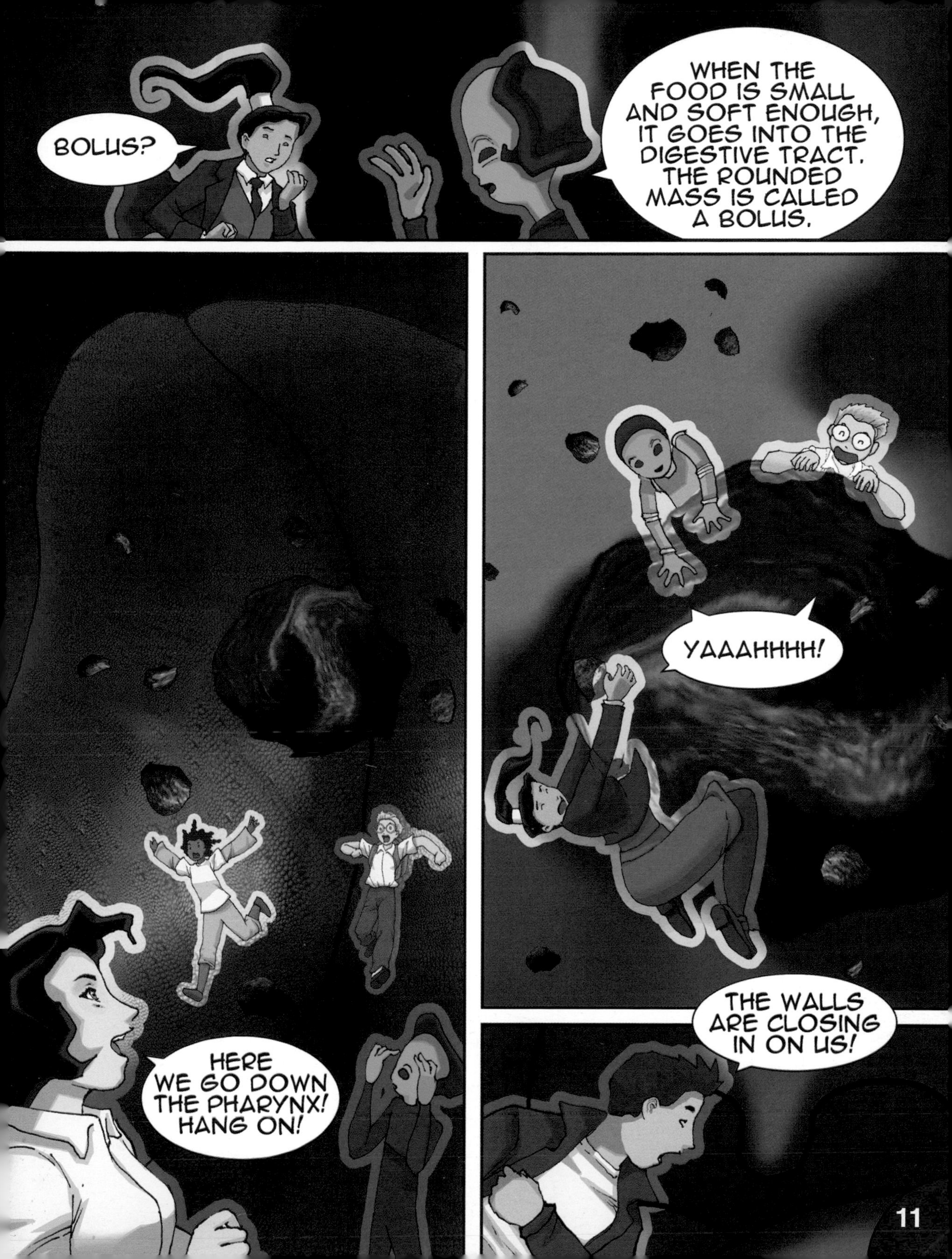
BOLUS?
WHEN THE FOOD IS SMALL AND SOFT ENOUGH, IT GOES INTO THE DIGESTIVE TRACT. THE ROUNDED MASS IS CALLED A BOLUS.
HERE WE GO DOWN THE PHARYNX! HANG ON!
YAAAHHHH!
THE WALLS ARE CLOSING IN ON US!

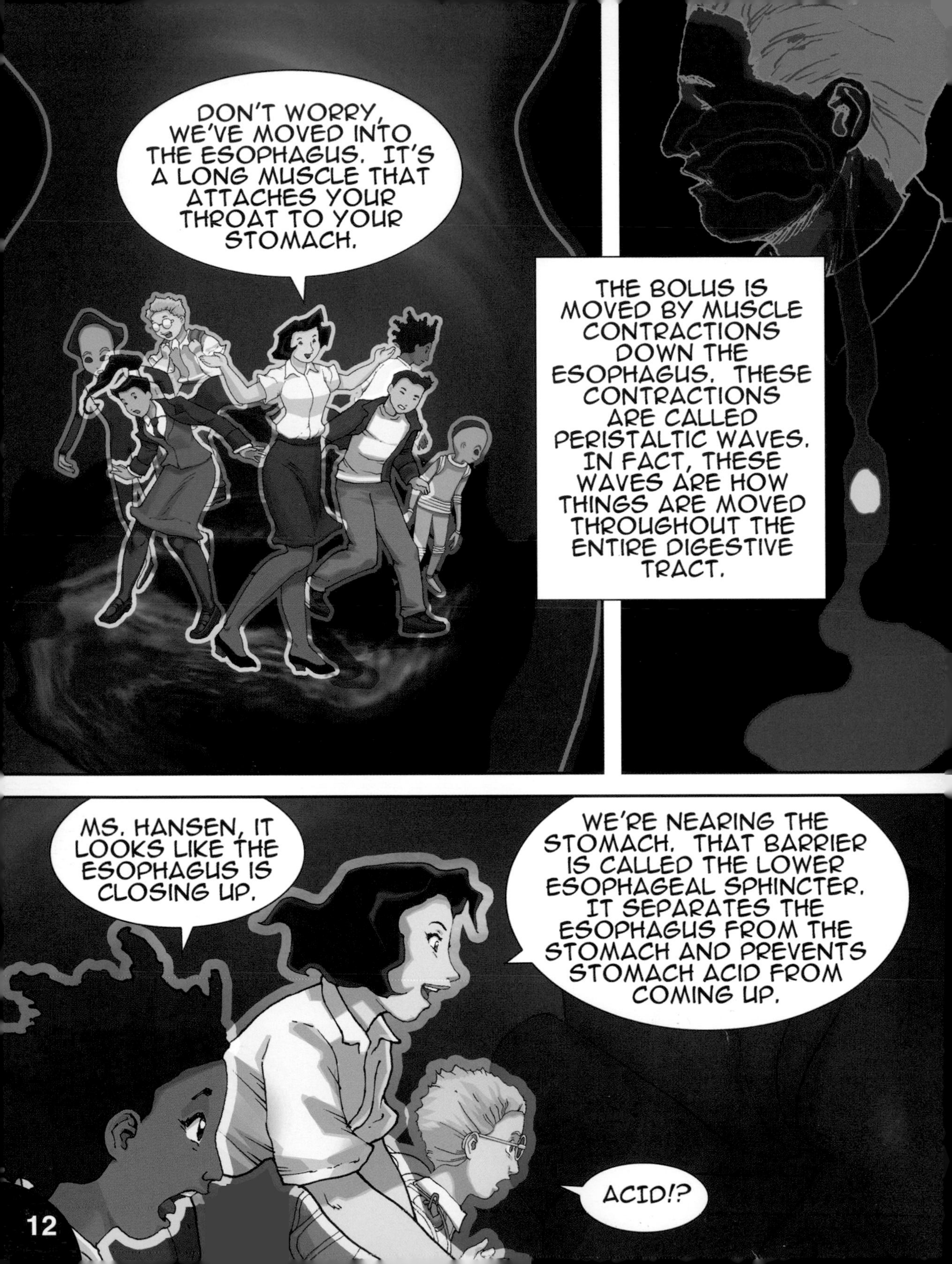
DON'T WORRY, WE'VE MOVED INTO THE ESOPHAGUS. IT'S A LONG MUSCLE THAT ATTACHES YOUR THROAT TO YOUR STOMACH.
THE BOLUS IS MOVED BY MUSCLE CONTRACTIONS DOWN THE ESOPHAGUS. THESE CONTRACTIONS ARE CALLED PERISTALTIC WAVES. IN FACT, THESE WAVES ARE HOW THINGS ARE MOVED THROUGHOUT THE ENTIRE DIGESTIVE TRACT.
MS. HANSEN, IT LOOKS LIKE THE ESOPHAGUS IS CLOSING UP.
WE'RE NEARING THE STOMACH. THAT BARRIER IS CALLED THE LOWER ESOPHAGEAL SPHINCTER. IT SEPARATES THE ESOPHAGUS FROM THE STOMACH AND PREVENTS STOMACH ACID FROM COMING UP.
ACID!?

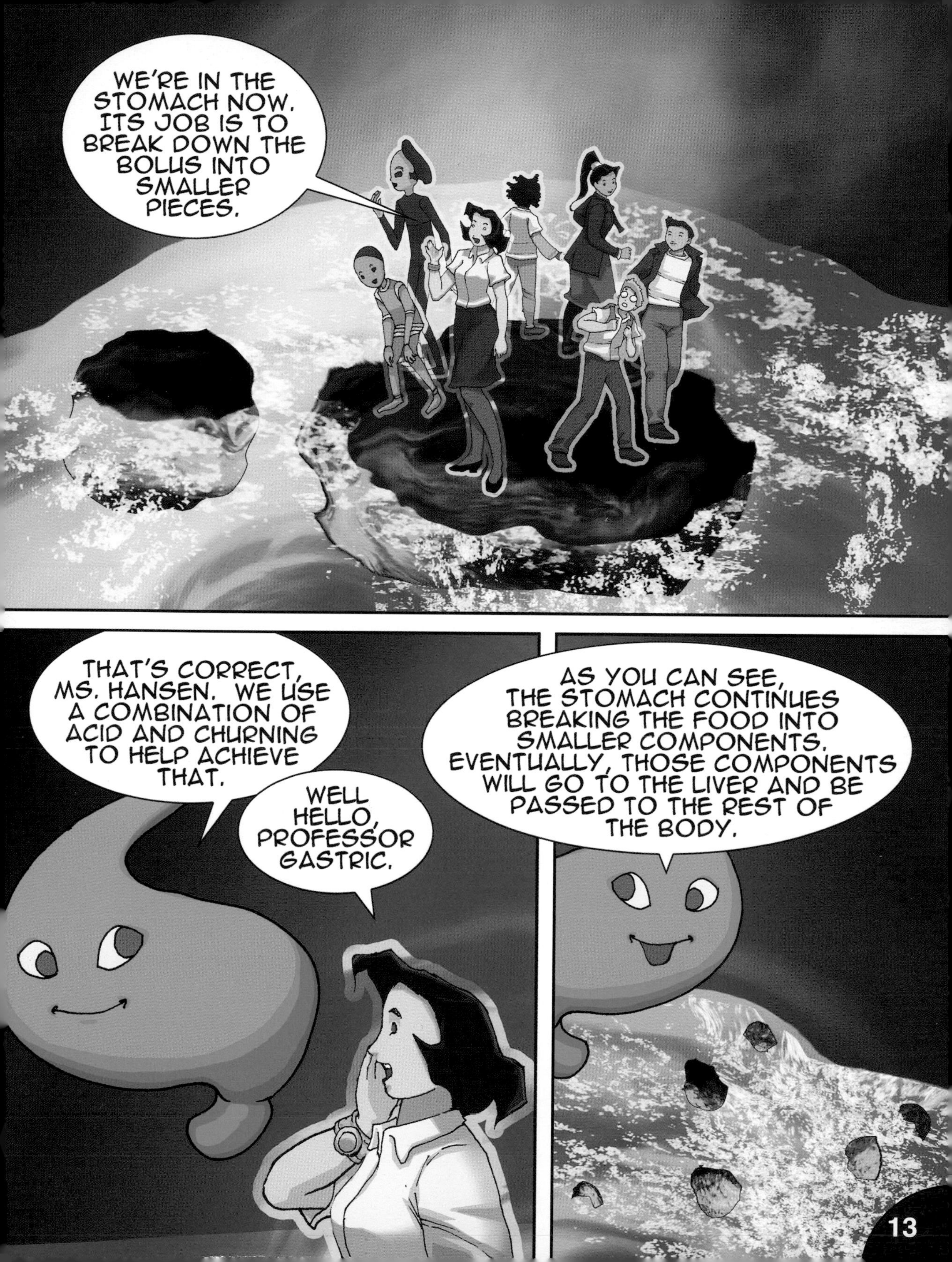
WE'RE IN THE STOMACH NOW. ITS JOB IS TO BREAK DOWN THE BOLUS INTO SMALLER PIECES.
THAT'S CORRECT, MS. HANSEN. WE USE A COMBINATION OF ACID AND CHURNING TO HELP ACHIEVE THAT.
WELL HELLO, PROFESSOR GASTRIC.
AS YOU CAN SEE, THE STOMACH CONTINUES BREAKING THE FOOD INTO SMALLER COMPONENTS. EVENTUALLY, THOSE COMPONENTS WILL GO TO THE LIVER AND BE PASSED TO THE REST OF THE BODY.

WHY DOESN'T THE ACID EAT THROUGH THE STOMACH?

IT HAS A SPECIAL LINING OF CELLS THAT PROTECTS IT.

TIME TO GO, KIDS. WE CAN'T STAY IN THIS ENVIRONMENT TOO LONG.

WHERE TO NEXT?

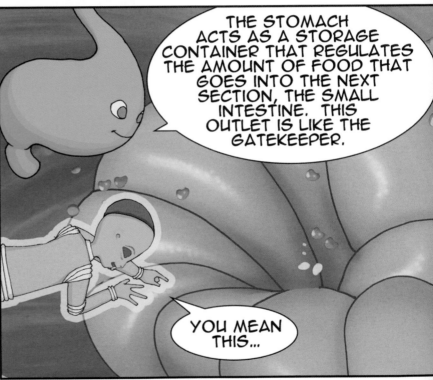

THE STOMACH ACTS AS A STORAGE CONTAINER THAT REGULATES THE AMOUNT OF FOOD THAT GOES INTO THE NEXT SECTION, THE SMALL INTESTINE. THIS OUTLET IS LIKE THE GATEKEEPER.

YOU MEAN THIS...

XENI!

I'M FINE...NO DAMAGE DONE.

WATCH WHERE YOU'RE GOING.

WE ARE NOW IN THE FIRST PART OF THE SMALL INTESTINE, CALLED THE DUODENUM. FROM HERE, WE'RE GOING TO VISIT THE LIVER.

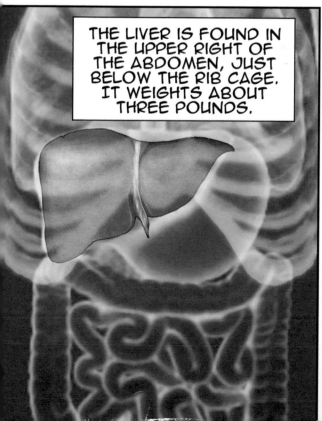

THE LIVER IS FOUND IN THE UPPER RIGHT OF THE ABDOMEN, JUST BELOW THE RIB CAGE. IT WEIGHTS ABOUT THREE POUNDS.

IT IS THE LARGEST GLAND OF THE BODY, ABOUT THE SIZE A FOOTBALL.

15

NOW WE ARE GOING TO THE LIVER BY GOING BACKWARD THROUGH THE BILE DUCT.

ONE OF THE MAIN FUNCTIONS OF THE LIVER IS TO PRODUCE BILE. BILE IS A SPECIAL FLUID.

gallbladder

BILE HAS TWO MAIN FUNCTIONS. FIRST, IT HELPS BREAK DOWN FOODS THAT WE EAT. SECOND, IT MOVES SOME OF THE WASTE THE LIVER MAKES INTO THE INTESTINE. WHEN BILE IS PRODUCED, IT IS STORED IN AN ORGAN CALLED THE GALLBLADDER AND THEN RELEASED WHENEVER NEEDED.

LET'S PREPARE TO GO UP THE DUCT.

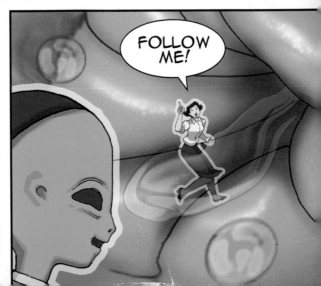

FOLLOW ME!

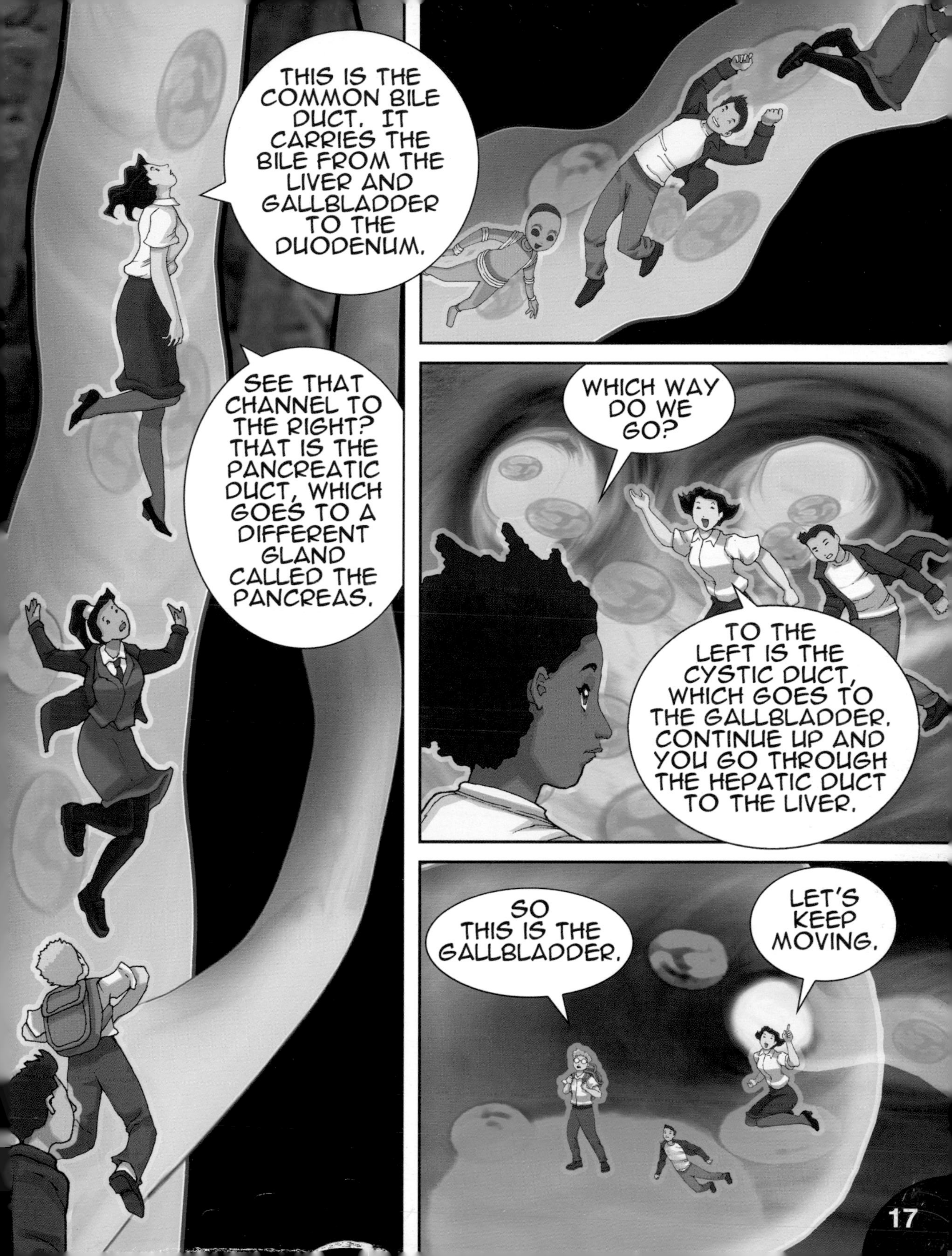
THIS IS THE COMMON BILE DUCT. IT CARRIES THE BILE FROM THE LIVER AND GALLBLADDER TO THE DUODENUM.
SEE THAT CHANNEL TO THE RIGHT? THAT IS THE PANCREATIC DUCT, WHICH GOES TO A DIFFERENT GLAND CALLED THE PANCREAS.
WHICH WAY DO WE GO?
TO THE LEFT IS THE CYSTIC DUCT, WHICH GOES TO THE GALLBLADDER. CONTINUE UP AND YOU GO THROUGH THE HEPATIC DUCT TO THE LIVER.
SO THIS IS THE GALLBLADDER.
LET'S KEEP MOVING.

ANOTHER BRANCH...WHERE TO NOW?

EACH ONE OF THESE DUCTS GOES TO A DIFFERENT PART OF THE LIVER.

THE LIVER IS DIVIDED INTO LEFT AND RIGHT SIDES, OR LOBES. THE RIGHT LOBE IS LARGER THAN THE LEFT. SPECIAL LIGAMENTS DIVIDE THE LIVER INTO SECTIONS.

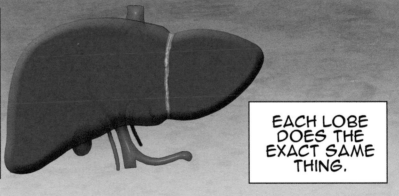

EACH LOBE DOES THE EXACT SAME THING.

WOW!

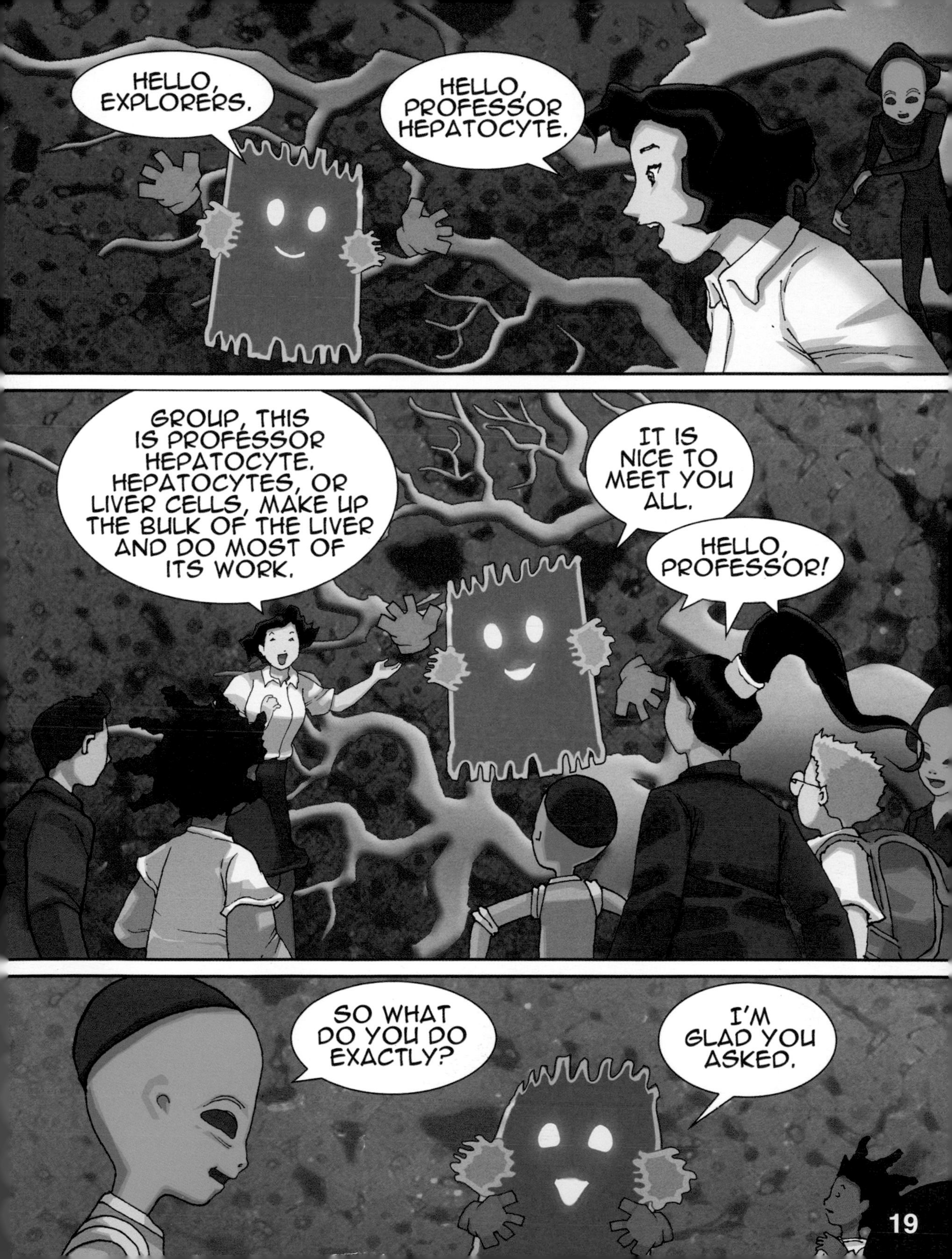
HELLO, EXPLORERS.
HELLO, PROFESSOR HEPATOCYTE.
GROUP, THIS IS PROFESSOR HEPATOCYTE. HEPATOCYTES, OR LIVER CELLS, MAKE UP THE BULK OF THE LIVER AND DO MOST OF ITS WORK.
IT IS NICE TO MEET YOU ALL.
HELLO, PROFESSOR!
SO WHAT DO YOU DO EXACTLY?
I'M GLAD YOU ASKED.

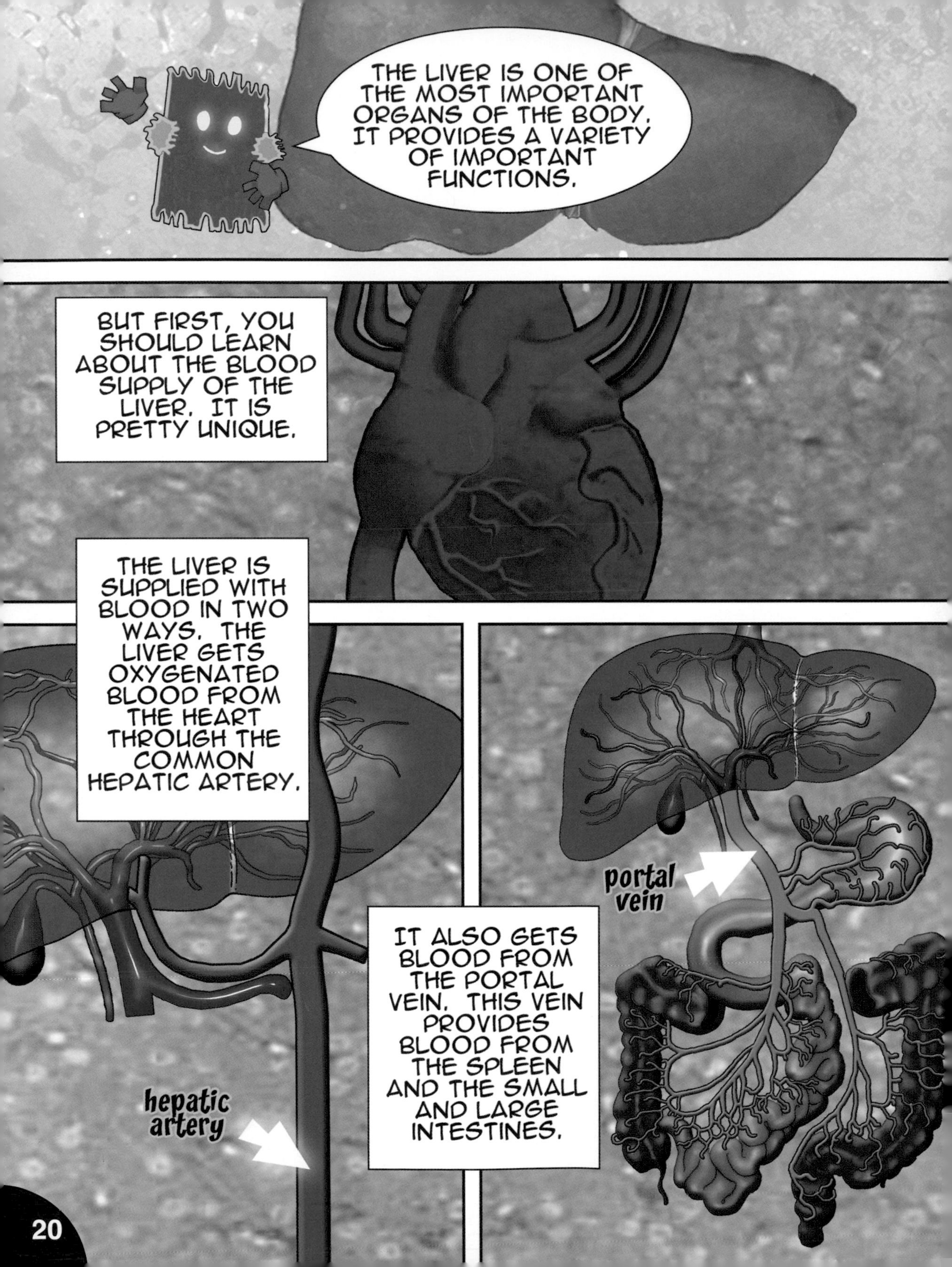

THE LIVER IS ONE OF THE MOST IMPORTANT ORGANS OF THE BODY. IT PROVIDES A VARIETY OF IMPORTANT FUNCTIONS.

BUT FIRST, YOU SHOULD LEARN ABOUT THE BLOOD SUPPLY OF THE LIVER. IT IS PRETTY UNIQUE.

THE LIVER IS SUPPLIED WITH BLOOD IN TWO WAYS. THE LIVER GETS OXYGENATED BLOOD FROM THE HEART THROUGH THE COMMON HEPATIC ARTERY.

hepatic artery

IT ALSO GETS BLOOD FROM THE PORTAL VEIN. THIS VEIN PROVIDES BLOOD FROM THE SPLEEN AND THE SMALL AND LARGE INTESTINES.

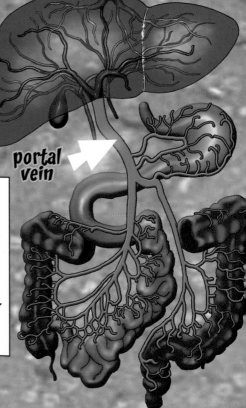

portal vein

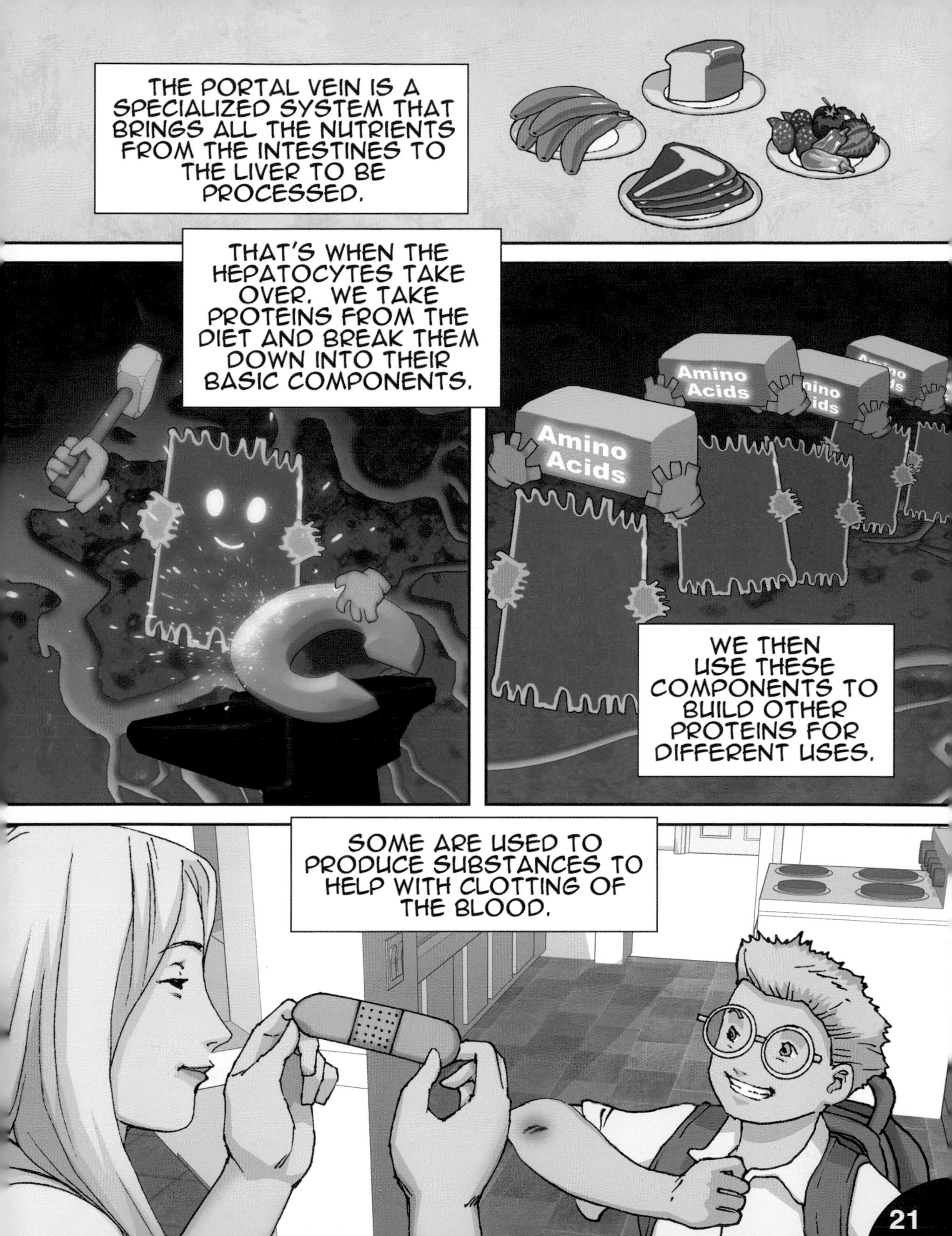
THE PORTAL VEIN IS A SPECIALIZED SYSTEM THAT BRINGS ALL THE NUTRIENTS FROM THE INTESTINES TO THE LIVER TO BE PROCESSED.
THAT'S WHEN THE HEPATOCYTES TAKE OVER. WE TAKE PROTEINS FROM THE DIET AND BREAK THEM DOWN INTO THEIR BASIC COMPONENTS.
Amino Acids
Amino Acids
WE THEN USE THESE COMPONENTS TO BUILD OTHER PROTEINS FOR DIFFERENT USES.
SOME ARE USED TO PRODUCE SUBSTANCES TO HELP WITH CLOTTING OF THE BLOOD.

ANOTHER IMPORTANT JOB WE DO IS HELP CONVERT CARBOHYDRATES TO SUGARS THAT THE BODY CAN USE.

AND AS YOU HAVE ALREADY SEEN, WE PRODUCE THE BILE THAT CAN BE USED TO BREAK DOWN THE FATS THAT WE EAT.

THAT'S PRETTY IMPRESSIVE.

WAIT... THAT'S NOT ALL.

WHEN THE RED BLOOD CELLS OF THE BODY BECOME OLDER, THE LIVER BREAKS THEM DOWN INTO CHEMICALS. THEN, THEY GET RELEASED IN THE BILE.

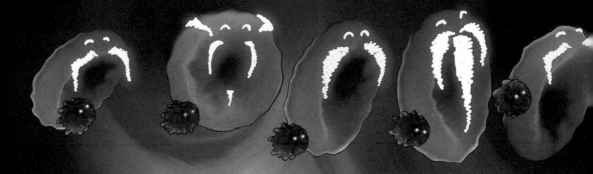

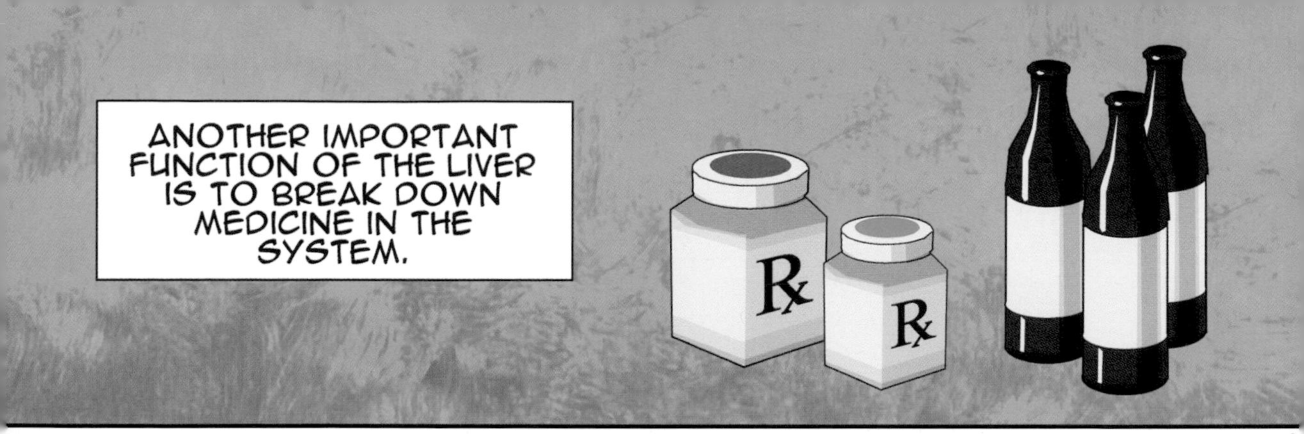
ANOTHER IMPORTANT FUNCTION OF THE LIVER IS TO BREAK DOWN MEDICINE IN THE SYSTEM.
Rx
Rx

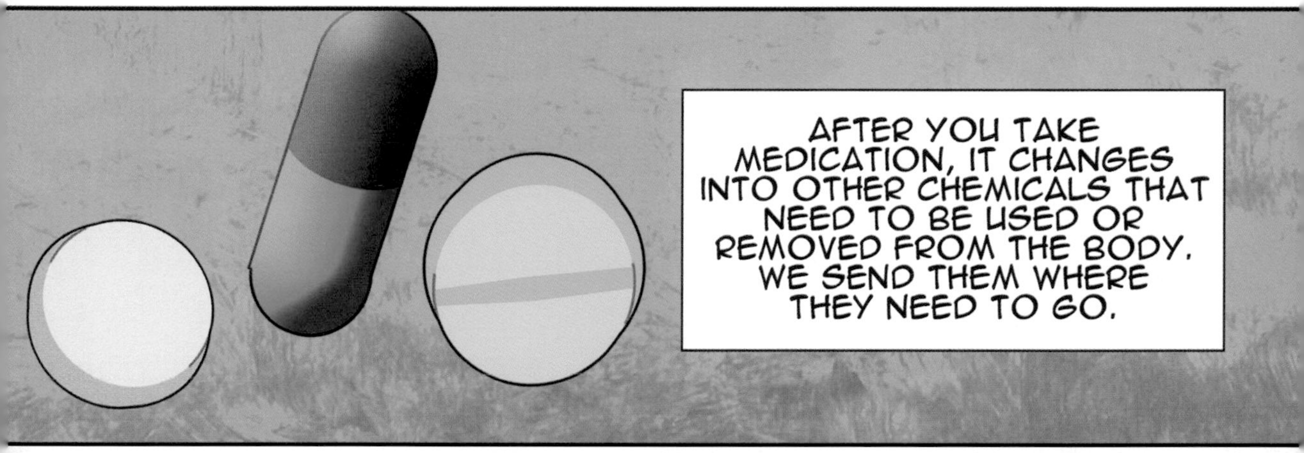
AFTER YOU TAKE MEDICATION, IT CHANGES INTO OTHER CHEMICALS THAT NEED TO BE USED OR REMOVED FROM THE BODY. WE SEND THEM WHERE THEY NEED TO GO.

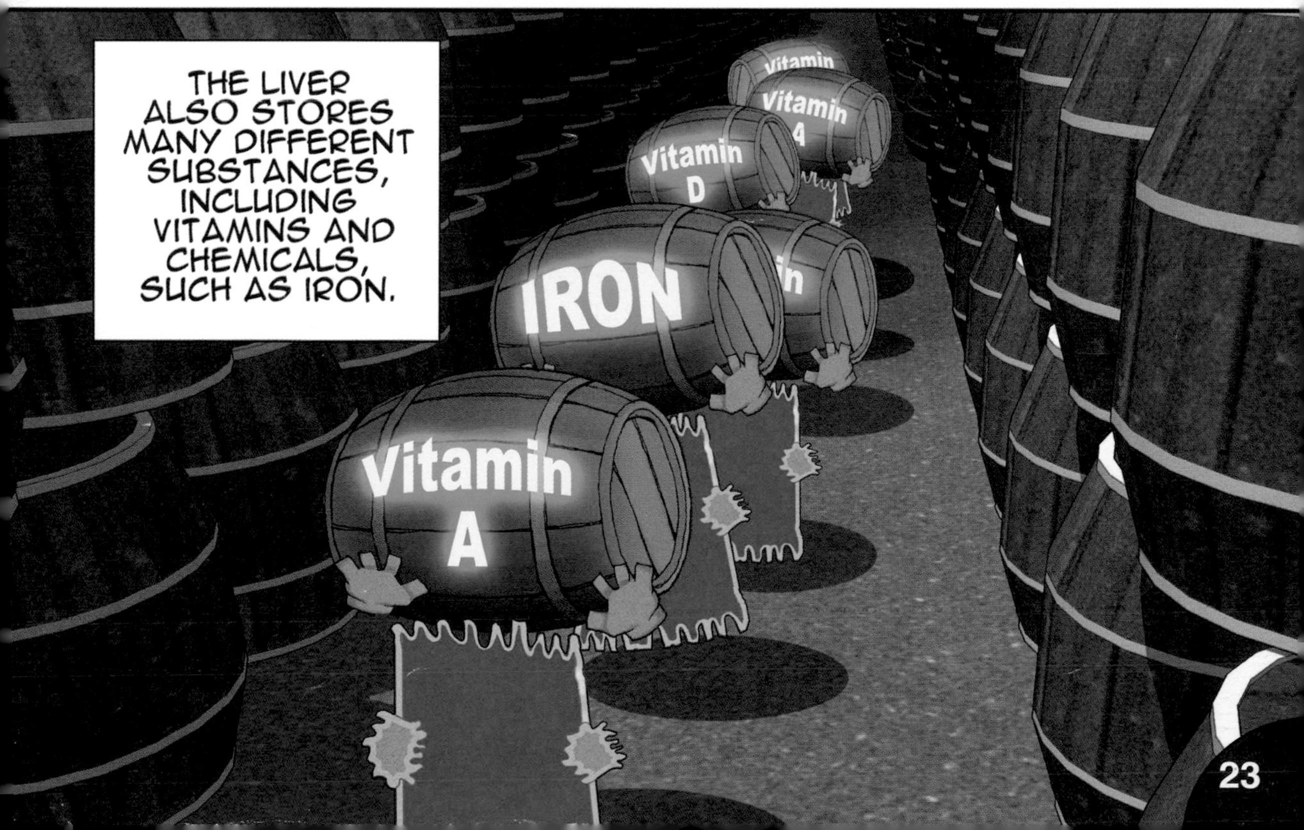
THE LIVER ALSO STORES MANY DIFFERENT SUBSTANCES, INCLUDING VITAMINS AND CHEMICALS, SUCH AS IRON.
Vitamin
Vitamin A
Vitamin D
IRON
Vitamin A

BECAUSE OF THE WORK THE LIVER DOES, IT IS QUITE TOUGH.

IF THE ORGAN IS DAMAGED, A SMALL PORTION CAN DO THE WORK OF THE ENTIRE LIVER.

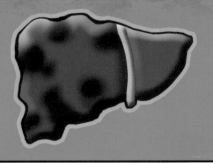

AND THE LIVER IS CAPABLE OF CREATING NEW CELLS TO REPLACE DAMAGED ONES.

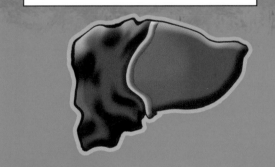

LOOK AT THE TIME! I HAVE TO TAKE MY LEAVE NOW. I HOPE YOU HAD A GOOD VISIT.

THANK YOU FOR YOUR TIME.

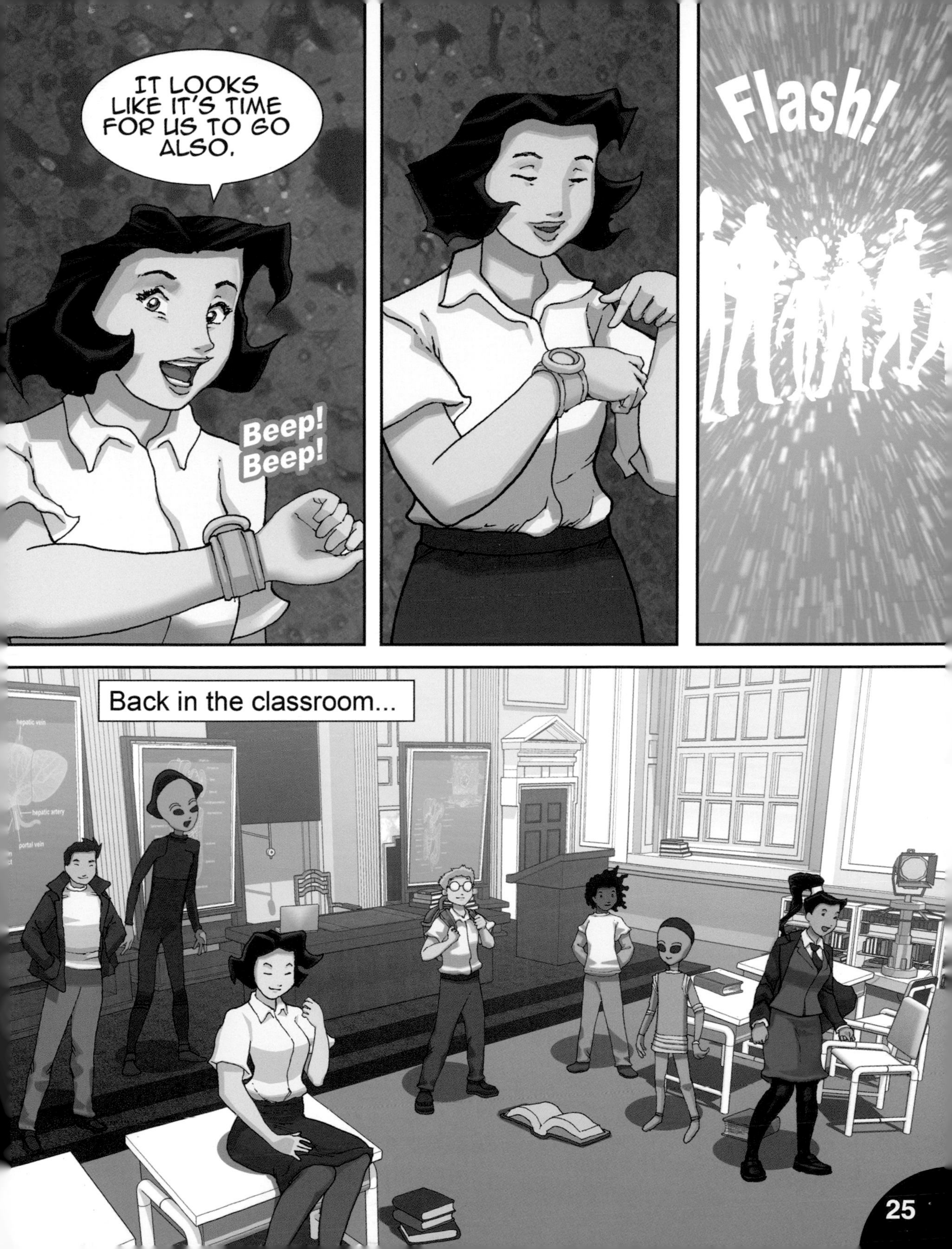
IT LOOKS LIKE IT'S TIME FOR US TO GO ALSO.
Beep! Beep!
Flash!
Back in the classroom...
hepatic vein
hepatic artery
portal vein

WOW! THE LIVER DOES A LOT OF THINGS.

IT SURE DOES. IT CAN BE DESCRIBED AS A MULTITASKER.

SO IT'S VERY IMPORTANT TO TAKE CARE OF THE LIVER.

ALCOHOL, FOR INSTANCE, CAN CAUSE DAMAGE AND SCAR THE LIVER. THE MOST SEVERE CASE OF THIS TYPE OF DAMAGE IS CALLED CIRRHOSIS.

MANY MEDICATIONS, EVEN THOSE THAT ARE QUITE COMMON, CAN DAMAGE THE LIVER AND SHOULD BE TAKEN WITH CAUTION.

CERTAIN CHEMICALS, SOME OF WHICH CAN ENTER THE BODY THROUGH THE LUNGS AND SKIN, CAN ALSO DAMAGE THE LIVER. SO, PLEASE, WATCH YOUR EXPOSURE TO ANY TYPE OF CHEMICALS.

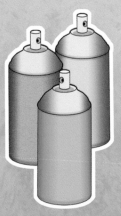

AND CERTAINLY AVOID SMOKING.

TO HELP TAKE CARE OF YOUR LIVER, MAKE SURE YOU DRINK LOTS OF WATER.

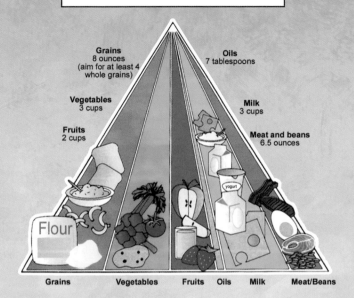

Grains
8 ounces
(aim for at least 4 whole grains)

Oils
7 tablespoons

Vegetables
3 cups

Milk
3 cups

Fruits
2 cups

Meat and beans
6.5 ounces

Flour

yogurt

Grains   Vegetables   Fruits   Oils   Milk   Meat/Beans

AND IT IS ALWAYS HELPFUL TO EAT A HEALTHY, BALANCED MEAL WHILE WATCHING HOW MUCH SUGAR AND FAT YOU CONSUME.

AN INTERESTING JOURNEY, AS USUAL.

THANK YOU FOR VISITING.

UNTIL NEXT TIME.

BYE!

The Liver: A Diagram

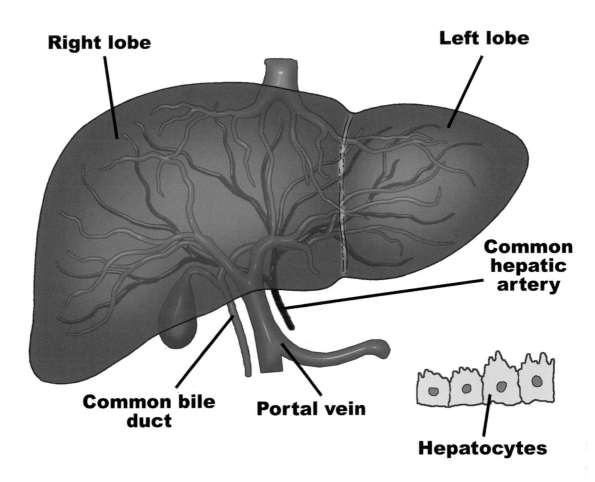

Right lobe

Left lobe

Common hepatic artery

Common bile duct

Portal vein

Hepatocytes

Fun Facts

The liver is the largest organ in the body. But it is 96 percent water!

Our journey took the Explorers up the duct that carries bile away from the liver. Normally, food enters the small intestine and is broken down to liquid. It is then absorbed into the blood and taken to the liver in the portal vein. The nutrients are taken from the blood in the liver. Then, they are sent where they are needed or stored. The liver sends more bile and waste to the gallbladder, which releases it back into the small intestine to go through the rest of digestion!

A common sign of liver disease is called jaundice. This is when a person's skin and the whites of the eyes are a yellow color. Jaundice occurs when the liver isn't able to process a reddish-yellow pigment called bilirubin.

Many babies have a form of jaundice because their livers can't process all the bilirubin. Did you have jaundice as a baby? How long did it take to go away?

Glossary

abdomen – the part of your body between the chest and the pelvis.

absorb – to take something in.

bacteria – tiny, one-celled organisms that can only be seen through a microscope.

component – a part of something; an ingredient.

digestive system – the system of organs that perform the breakdown of food into substances small enough for the body to absorb. The mouth, stomach, liver, and intestines are part of this system.

nutrient – a substance found in food and used in the body to promote growth, maintenance, and repair.

pharynx – the muscular tube from the mouth and nose to the esophagus. The pharynx is also called the throat.

unique – being the only one of its kind.

Web Sites

To learn more about the liver, visit ABDO Group online at **www.abdopublishing.com**. Web sites about the liver are featured on our Book Links page. These links are routinely monitored and updated to provide the most current information available.

About the Author

Joeming Dunn is both a general practice physician and the owner of one of the largest comic companies in Texas, Antarctic Press. A graduate of Austin College in Sherman and the University of Texas Medical Branch in Galveston, Dunn has currently settled in San Antonio.

Dr. Dunn has written or co-authored texts in both the medical and graphic novel fields. He met his wife, Teresa, in college, and they have two bright and lovely girls, Ashley and Camerin. Ashley has even helped some with his research for these Magic Wagon books.

About the Illustrator

Rod Espinosa is a graphic novel creator, writer, and illustrator. Espinosa was born in the Philippines in Manila. He graduated from the Don Bosco Technical College and the University of Santo Tomas.

Espinosa has worked in advertising, software entertainment, and film. Today, he lives in San Antonio, Texas, and produces stunning graphic novels including *Dinowars, Neotopia, Metadocs, Battle Girlz, Alice in Wonderland, Stop TB!,* and *Prince of Heroes.* His graphic novel *Courageous Princess* was nominated for an Eisner Award.

Index

A

acid 12, 13, 14

B

bile 16, 17, 22
blood 20, 21, 22
bolus 10, 11, 12, 13

C

carbohydrate 22
cirrhosis 26
common bile duct 16, 17
common hepatic artery 20
cystic duct 17

D

duodenum 15, 17

E

esophagus 12

G

gallbladder 16, 17

H

hepatic duct 17
hepatocyte 19, 21

L

large intestine 20
left lobe 18
ligament 18
lower esophageal sphincter 12

P

pancreas 17
pancreatic duct 17
papillae 9
peristaltic waves 12
pharynx 11
portal vein 20, 21
protection 26, 27

R

rib cage 15
right lobe 18

S

saliva 10
small intestine 14, 15, 20
stomach 12, 13, 14
spleen 20

T

teeth 9
tongue 9